Light A Fire

By BeeKels ArtOrigins

"Light A Fire" is poetic, describing a Girl's First, and what leads to A Woman's Reflection. BeeKels ArtOrigins describes a world of woman and man. The mindfulness that a young woman has when making choices made to ignite a relationship start with a single ember. The poetic fire builds, with timbers that describe trial and error that continues throughout a love story.

Light A Fire

Table of Contents

Prologue: Introduction to the Fire Pit

Section 1: A Glimmer of Hope

Section 2: A Lit Match

Section 3: A Blaze

Section 4: Fire

Section 5: It Is Smoking

Section 6: Another Match

Part Two

Section 7: Adding Tinder

Section 8: Brilliant Flame

Introduction to the Fire Pit

A girl's firsts...

The bliss of finally enjoying

themselves

With just them

With another

And finding someone new

Remember that first sexy character from your first erotic book?

Remember your first kiss?

Remember how you felt after slapping that boy in first grade who insulted your pink tutu?

Remember how your first purchase went?

Remember that feeling when you bought your first set of lingerie?

Remember how wine nights and nights on the prowl went?

Remember that first happy thought of

"yes"?

Remember how "you" became the

gorgeous person that you are?

A Glimmer of Hope

Sailing To Sleep

The problem is that I cannot get you out

of my head.

You are like a bad dream

Or a melody from my favorite song.

Melancholy like the blues or sweet like

cream,

You drift in and out.

Filled with mercury we separate

And go our different ways.

Like a ball of string,

Wind round and round

And being

Close together becomes complicated.

Like in the music that I listen to at night

Your voice is carried in waves

My mind set tranquil

And with, I fell

Peace in heart

And I sail to sleep

The gypsy breaks the ground

With tap and stomp

My fire is lit and

A blaze in brought forth

Salvaging the last bit of sound,

Of reason to stay and watch

You play your heart out

I linger

Beauty is in your eyes

When you play

A fire gleams like the kind

Gold piece on my mantel,

On your hearth

Too Skinny?

Everyone is doing it.

Do not you know.

Bra and underwear in my hand

Stepping off, my foot

Leaves land

Into a pool of water to feel

A rush of energy under the sun

The warm water and me, lots of fun.

School Codified Language

How will I approach;

Will my point even get across your

Big, wide surface?

--your face that is such a mystery

To analyze

For it gives away not a hint

Of emotion or brief expression

Of thought.

A Lit Match

Teenage me: Ojos Asi, pretty sure my version is better Shakira!

It is only in your eyes,

With colours that are pure and seductive

That make me plunge into a deep abyss

Of feeling,

Where I can find love... peace.

Aplomb, perfect in extraordinary ways,

Presents itself as absent

Each time I am sunken into

Those window that lead me

To a path so straight.

Reading Between the Lines

My first instinct was

To say no, but then I would wonder.

Taking a change and saying

"Yes"

Was something impulsive

Do I mean it now?

So will we wait…

And what if tomorrow

Is not promised

Do we sit and ponder

While our hearts hum?

Truth be told

I was wishing

For someone new

Just to take my mind

Off of the one

Who I had been

Thinking of.

A Blaze

You're Crushing It

You confuse me

You make me feel inferior

To every move, to every

Step you take

Equal of different so much

That it will matter, I feel that it

Will be best

To try and figure you out

And see if you'll meet

Me half way

Stay away and I will wait

As long as my heart is full

Of your melodic voice and

My rhythms—collide.

We've been sitting here

Anticipating every inch of warmth

That would fill our hearts,

But what we've failed to realize

Was that

We were not smart enough

To turn on

The love already in the hearth

Fire

Initiation

Do we sit and ponder while our heart

hum?

Do we spread our wings

And leave the cage

Of fear behind?

In the summer I dreamed an us

Kissing in the moonlight

I try new things

When I am curious

To learn and absorb

A new form of knowledge

Is my only goal

In the fall I felt your

Arms tanned by a sun's rays

I'm not asking you to

Judge me when I do not

Try something new

It's just who I choose

To be

In the winter my heart was cold

All over but yet you let me into our

Loving gaze

So call it a crime

That I question a lot

And try to

Reach for more

And despite lack of desire

To try or engage

In something that goes

Against may morals

I still find life intriguing

And full of purpose

In spring my heart danced

Even when you weren't by me

Connected were we by an invisible line

Torn...

Torn from us forever,

Never to return

Or can we now sit

Side by side?

Puppy and Love?

It gets header to tell whether

Or not I am enamored with you still

Day by day

I wonder why, and then

I look up and you have gone away

My burden gets harder to bear

As I look inside my heart

So I wait until I have seen

Your face again so my heart will restart

My number on your cell phone

A phone tag before a date

A rainy night of driving

Or a taxi while I wait

Walking out of your apartment

So cold I feel without you near

I want to know if you are sincere

I am not one to be playing

Not one to fall and not love again

My question is this though

Do I not deserve to be kissed or missed?

It is Smoking Hot

Moist

Like in my hair, water drips

From the leaves

Like my eyelids, the branches droop

Ever so slightly

Like a deer, the drops of rain scurry

Down a path on my window

Like a game, they race

Til they reach the finish line

Like a drum, thunder echoes

Throughout the forest

Like an animal of prey, I wait

Are you on the hunt tonight?

I am pretty sure that

Heels, makeup, and a tight dress

Are code for torture.

I do not even know you.

Yet, I agreed.

A date, no leash attached.

No whistle while you work agreement.

Just us.

One night, drinks out.

And vent.

You're Puzzling

I cannot read your face.

What does it even say?!

Do you want me to go

Or do you want me to stay?

Question your life, woman.

Am I even capable of reading

such a puzzle as you?

In your heart, I wonder

Is there room for two?

End of the Walk of Shame

I'm out of bandages

For my battle scars

I let them fester

And hurt for all to see

I am tired of beating

Myself my heart to death

While I question what

Went wrong and whether it was me

Back for Misery

Toying with my glass full of liquor

The stem of a cherry more appetizing

Can I even do tricks?

My tongue tied

As you sit next to me.

Nah? I hate that character.

I am bold. I am brass. I am kicking butt tonight!

Walk me home, and be my man for tonight.

To chance it I ask you

Straight to your face

Is it me?

Or do you possibly just want to cave?

Romance me with your heart

Or so you say

Why do you not talk

It makes me want to

Keep away.

Lonely as I feel

Will you ever know

Night Two: Wing Man

You're attractive. That's why I brought you along.

You're not mine.

I am wearing this dress you approved of.

I am perfectly tame. No boys milling around.

Your posture; are you trying

To keep me away?

Or are you saving

Your love for a rainy day?

It's my last time taking you with me.

The bar is too quite.

I found him in the crowd tonight,

He is quite foine... hot...

Tempting me to sin on this bar.... stool

His gaze leaves me

Nervous

But you are still next to me.

My "friend" who happens to ignore

The womanly curves of this dress

So I end up watching and waiting.

My stalking on a bar stool approach

Never worked

You are not interested in men.

Protection, solidarity on bar stool.

Maybe, I was blessed.

I think it's interesting enough

That you ogle me still

I find it hard enough

To have the will

To stand there and endure

While you sit with your guys

Or pretend that I am happy

While you play with your toys

Cats toy with their food.

And I am all homo sapien: Female

Disinterested and off to hunt somewhere else.

Another Match

What if I told you

That you were not alone

They had been there and back

Cut yourself some slack

Although it is still there

Hold on to the fact

That there is still time

For love to unwind

Your elder sisters, mothers, and cousins

Have wisdom.

Your father figures do, too.

Though rejection or lust is harmful

There is repentance, healing

You will be a freer you.

Peace stops even the most troubled of

heart.

Entwined is a Word

Time is a human concept

And I am still searching

For that person

To spend with

All of me.

This is our song.

Like a whirlwind, my pain cycled

Through my being and what I knew

To be true

About myself

Was mangled and bruised.

I had to wait for my Heavenly Father

To show me

Again.

How I was forgiven for my sins,

But that my enemy

Still needed to

Be forgiven as well.

Part Two

A Woman

It is hard to recognize myself in the

mirror

The woman

With doe eyes and

A streak of burgundy

With a tattoo in tow

What does my physical appearance

Say about the soul,

And the heart?

2 Timothy 1:7

No Fear.

Bar Crawl: Yes, I College

My Conscious

I told you not to go out with your girls tonight.

Passing out at one thirty in the a.m.

Eyeliner smudges one my zebra print pillow

I fell today. I think that's what that rip on my jeans means.

Two hours later, still trying to sleep.
Passed out at five in the a.m.

Oh, look! I have an eight in the a.m. course in the [insert your class that you know that you failed as soon as you walk into the door and look at the rest of your classmates and see them snoring or holding their coffee cups for dear

life in the first row of a lecture course that you actually need to pass in order to get to the upper level courses in your major!!!!]
Go me!

Does angst extend into college years?
Because I think that it does.

I wanted to shout at him
Tell him exactly what was going through my head.

It was the man-boy who smiled at me
In Spanish class

Feigned to know anything about the language

It's college, you should know a word or two!
"Hey, I still like you so do not break my heart!"

But yet again, like you said
"it was all inside my head"
Talking to my friend made it easier
We had all gone through it before.

I can't believe crushes still exist in college…

Talking out the pain

Made it easier to bear

The jealousy still hurt

Me still hurt

Me

As I watch you

"move on"

Vied For

The curves with tan lines

Like Luke Bryant in a head shot

Did not exactly do it for me that night

I needed a little more.

And the books

Peeking

At me

From the bottom of the bookshelf

With the lines of anticipation

(insert ROCKY quote here)

And desire

I need to call my boyfriend

And listen to his voice.

All the Way Back to Zero

It was not like I had not

Had not make the speech to myself before

Something about:

A higher calling

A humility issue

So instead of finding this wisdom,

You exhibited the character of a godly man.

Who knew that under all of that pride

You had a heart?

A good guy friend is hard to find.

Yes, you can hold my hand as we walk down the street. Yes, you can tell me the truth, when I am stubborn. Yes, you can encourage me to be my best—to study!

We had a civil conversation, while inside all
I wanted was to hurt you for exhorting me to be better,
To be a godly me.

Your eyes danced when you laughed

With me.

That laugh was genuine.

The dove look both left and right

When in flight

He rises above the world

He takes no sides

Gliding in and out of glory's channels

Of light.

One can definitely see

That He has a purpose.

Adding Tinder

It's a trying thing, this game of Life

You have to go through troubles
To end up right side up.

Man who is attractive, and pursues.
We had a civil conversation.

We talk in person. We eat a bite of lunch.

You choose, this time to look me
In the eyes
And then say something and nothing
At the same time.

Until you choose to walk away

And we start at zero again.

Is that love to wipe

Someone's name off of a piece of paper

With an eraser

Because that might actually work better

Than me just

Staring at a piece of paper…

I am afraid to speak you to this time.

My feelings are strong, but

There is less validity

As you have developed feelings for

another

Walk beside them,

Instead of me.

All I see

in your painfully, beautiful eyes

Is hurt

It is, as if, I have done you

The greatest disservice of loving you

From a distance.

We ran to find what we wanted--

Our other half.

The beach seemed endless and very long.

It was love at first sight, and when we

Finally did see each other, we kissed each

other.

[An alarm clock chimes, time for another

eight in the a.m. course.]

So call it a crime

That I question a lot.

Like a cat in the night

My footsteps made no sound

Padding.

Time to watch movies with

My besties.

When life gives you lemons

You take those lemons

And run to a juicer!

Enjoy your lemonade!

Do not forget to add your sweetness.

By Yourself

You can Be Intelligent, Be Funny, and Be Charismatic

In Other People

You can find love, see a new you develop

Into a blossoming sun beam

Whose been hiding behind dark clouds.

Chase those clouds away!

Brilliant Flames

A woman's body is a temple.

A woman's body is one enormous

Sacrifice.

A vessel not to be taken lightly.

A woman's life is precious,

It is sacred.

She enters the world in a flood

Of bodily fluids

Is loved and cherished for the blood she

provides

Is enraptured by love

And is able to show

That same love in her body

Not a thing is like a woman's sacrifice.

Truth Be Told Women,

Love is a Jewel.

Life if For the Living,

And You

Choose to Live in the NOW!

This life is worth living

Truth Be Told

And You, yes You!

Will LIVE IT!

You will make mistakes,

Bump into walls,

But there is always an open window

Or door

For You to walk towards when You are

Done

And

Ready To Walk again and

Enjoy the Sunshine.

Thank you for reading

Light A Fire.

MORE ABOUT

THE AUTHOR

BeeKels

ArtOrigins

Kelsi B. Brooks (BeeKels ArtOrigins) is an Educator who resides in Atlanta, Georgia. She enjoys the performing arts, hiking outdoors, and bonding with animals. As a new author, she writes a historical fiction and a short story about the paranormal. The inner beauty of light is inspiration for BeeKels ArtOrigins. In her books, she seeks to illuminate truths of romance, historical ties to reality's past, and use fiction as her lamp.

The journey of freedom starts with a reason to be enslaved. When Tembo and his comrades flee to become a part of the Cimarron band, a new life can become a reality for runaway slaves. This historical fiction explores the narrative of

Native Indians in the South Eastern region. Enjoy her latest publication on Amazon, called "Light: A Historical Fiction".

https://authorbeekelsartorigins.wordpress.com/

Made in the USA
Columbia, SC
18 May 2020